Arnold and Louise

The Great Louweezie

by Erica S. Perl

illustrated by Chris Chatterton

Penguin Workshop

An Imprint of Penguin Random House

PENGUIN WORKSHOP
Penguin Young Readers Group
An Imprint of Penguin Random House LLC

Text copyright © 2019 by Erica S. Perl. Illustrations copyright © 2019 by Penguin Random House LLC. All rights reserved. Published by Penguin Workshop, an imprint of Penguin Random House LLC, 345 Hudson Street, New York, New York 10014. PENGUIN and PENGUIN WORKSHOP are trademarks of Penguin Books Ltd, and the W colophon is a registered trademark of Penguin Random House LLC. Manufactured in China.

Library of Congress Cataloging-in-Publication Data is available.

ISBN 9781524790394 (paperback)   10 9 8 7 6 5 4 3 2 1
ISBN 9781524790400 (library binding)   10 9 8 7 6 5 4 3 2 1

In memory of H. Billy Greene, a.k.a.
(The Great) Billgreeni—ESP

Chapter One

"Oh dear," said Arnold when he looked outside.

Arnold and his best friend, Louise, had been planning to have a picnic.

The dark clouds suggested otherwise.

Arnold went to Louise's house to tell her the bad news.

"Louise?" called Arnold.

"There is no one here by that name," said a voice.

"Louise?" Arnold asked again.

"I am NOT Louise," she said, storming out. "I am the Great Louweezie! I can predict the future."

Arnold raised an eyebrow.

"I came to tell you that we can't have our picnic today," he said. "It looks like rain."

"Today is not a day for picnics!" announced the Great Louweezie.

"Correct," said Arnold.

"Aha!" The Great Louweezie put

out her hand. "Ten cents, please."

Arnold shook his head.

"You don't have ten cents,"

said the Great Louweezie.

"I knew it! The Great

Louweezie sees all. The

Great Louweezie knows all."

"Okay, Your Greatness," said Arnold. "What am I thinking about now?"

Inside his pocket, his fingers found his lucky marble.

The Great Louweezie stared deep into Arnold's eyes.

What if she says "a marble"? Arnold wondered.

Reading minds? Predicting the future?

Arnold was pretty sure those things were impossible, even for the Great Louweezie.

Weren't they?

Chapter Two

The Great Louweezie looked
Arnold up and down.

"You're thinking about . . .
uh, a . . . star . . . jar . . .
car . . . mar . . ."

Arnold nodded expectantly
when he heard "mar."

"A car?"

"No," said Arnold.

"A carnival?"

"No."

"A carton of milk?"

"Close," said Arnold, to
make her feel better. "But no."

The Great Louweezie
stamped her foot.

"I told you!" she said.

"It doesn't work without the

ten cents."

"I could give you a marble," said Arnold.

He hadn't planned on offering it—all that thinking about it just made the word roll out of his mouth.

"Which marble?" asked the Great Louweezie. "Your big red shooter?"

"No." Arnold took his lucky marble out of his pocket,

regretting the offer already.

"But you have to actually

predict something. Something

that's going to happen to me
today."

"It's not a very big marble,"
said the Great Louweezie.

"Oh. Okay," said Arnold,
feeling relieved.

"But it is a nice color,"
the Great Louweezie added.
"So, it's a deal."

"It has to be a *real* prediction," said Arnold. "Not just that I'm going to sneeze, or something obvious like that."

Arnold sneezed a lot.

"It's a deal," repeated
the Great Louweezie.

Chapter Three

The Great

Louweezie

closed her eyes.

Then opened

them.

"You're too right-side-up."

Arnold lowered his hands to the ground.

He kicked his legs up toward the darkening sky.

The scent of wild onions tickled his nose.

"Perfect!" The Great
Louweezie closed her eyes
again.

"The Great Louweezie is getting something. It's still fuzzy . . . a cat . . . or maybe a dog . . ."

She opened her eyes.

"I forget. Where was I?"

"Cats . . . dogs . . ."

"Right! Cats and dogs, hats and frogs . . ."

Arnold felt a raindrop.

"Louise? It's starting to rain."

"Bats and logs . . ."

Another raindrop landed. In Arnold's upside-down nose.

"Achoo!" Arnold toppled

over.

THUD!

"Rain makes me sneeze," he muttered.

"Everything makes you sneeze," she said.

"I want my marble back,"

said Arnold. "I want to go home."

"You can't go! Please, give me one more chance."

Arnold sighed.

"Okay," she said. "The Great

Louweezie needs you to do . . .

this."

She spun in place.

Slowly, Arnold did the same.

"Faster! Now follow me!"

Chapter Four

The Great Louweezie ran

down to the creek.

She danced across it,

hopping from stone to stone.

Carefully, Arnold tried to

follow.

"And up, and then . . ." She took a flying leap off a big slippery rock.

Arnold made it to the big slippery rock.

But before he could jump to the next rock like the Great Louweezie, one foot slid out from under him.

Then the other. Then . . .

"Don't worry. I've got you,"

said the Great Louweezie,

guiding Arnold to dry land.

"And I've got *it*, too!"

"My marble?"

"No, silly! My prediction."

"Great," said Arnold. "Tell

me quickly so I can go home."

The Great Louweezie
grinned. She stood tall to
make her announcement.

"*Cats and dogs* meant it was going to *rain* cats and dogs. The Great Louweezie's prediction is that you are going to get wet and have fun!"

"For your information, I am already wet. And being wet is *not* my idea of fun," he said.

"So, the Great Louweezie is *half* right?"

"Marble," demanded Arnold.

Chapter Five

When Arnold got home, he
curled up in front of the fire.

When he woke up, he was
warm and dry.

Outside, rain was still

coming down. Hard.

Cats and dogs, Arnold thought.

He took out his marble and polished it.

It shone like a lucky marble.

It shone like a wet stone in a

creek.

It shone like his best friend's

eyes.

Arnold sighed.

He put the marble in his

pocket.

Then he went back outside.

"Great Louweezie?" he
called.

A sad voice answered,
"There is no one here by that
name."

Arnold peeked inside her

doorway.

"Louise! I'm glad I found

you. I have something for

you," Arnold said, holding out

his lucky marble.

Louise looked at the marble, then at her friend.

"The Great Louweezie's prediction came true," said Arnold.

"You're just saying that to make me feel better," said Louise.

"No, I'm not," insisted Arnold. "You were right. I did get wet.

"And then I took a nap in front of my fireplace. Which is what *I* do for fun.

"So, all the things you said would happen did. See?"

Louise brightened a little. "I think so."

"And now, I'm wet again.

But I'm also having fun,
because I always do when
I'm with my best friend," said
Arnold.

"You mean the Great Louweezie's prediction came true *twice*?" she said.

Arnold nodded.

"So, you're giving me *two* marbles?"

"Oh," said Arnold. "I guess so."

"It's okay—you can owe me one," offered Louise. "And maybe if it stops raining tomorrow, I could do some more predictions."

"How about we have a picnic instead?"

"Can I wear my cape?"

"Of course," said Arnold, pulling his head out.

Louise ran outside and

twirled excitedly.

"The Great Louweezie predicts that our picnic will be a fabulous success!"